For Joan

The publishers would like to thank
James Putnam for checking the facts in this book.

First U.S. edition 1996

Library of Congress Cataloging-in-Publication Data
Anderson, Scoular.
A puzzling day in the land of the Pharaohs / Scoular Anderson.
—1st U.S. ed.
Summary: While on a field trip to the museum to learn about
ancient Egypt, Mrs. Pudget's class searches for hidden objects and solves
puzzles in order to return to the present.
ISBN 1-56402-877-1
[1. School field trips—Fiction. 2. Egypt—Civilization—
To 332 B.C.—Fiction. 3. Picture puzzles.] I. Title.
PZ7.A5495Pw   1996
[E]—dc20   95-43949

2 4 6 8 10 9 7 5 3 1

Printed in Italy

This book was typeset in AT Amigo.
The pictures were done in watercolor.

Candlewick Press
2067 Massachusetts Avenue
Cambridge, Massachusetts 02140

A PUZZLING DAY IN
THE LAND OF THE PHARAOHS

SCOULAR ANDERSON

CANDLEWICK PRESS
CAMBRIDGE, MASSACHUSETTS

Welcome to ancient Egypt,
the land of the Pharaohs, O party of ten
from the Nile Street School. I am Thoth, god
of learning and magic.

With your audio tour cassette player and the Pharaoh's permission, I have brought you here to learn about our wonderful land. In exchange you must find special gifts for the Pharaoh's birthday, which is today.

If the Pharaoh is pleased with your gifts, he will allow you to return to the museum. But if he is not pleased, O party of ten, you will stay here and build pyramids until he permits you to leave.

Moaning minnows! I'm sure I'm not meant to be here. I'd better keep out of sight. I must get back to the museum, but how? I know! I need the cassette player and a special gift for the Pharaoh's birthday. I'll steal them from the Nile Street School bunch!
Oh, no! Mr. Gluddery's here, too.
I told you it was the Pharaoh's birthday.
Phew! It's hot here.

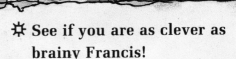

Reader!
You may also travel in the land of the Pharaohs. But I have some tasks for you. At each place we visit you must:

- **Help one of the party of ten find a special gift for the Pharaoh's birthday.**
- **Count the gifts found so far to make sure none is lost.**
- **Find out who has the cassette player. Without it, the party of ten will not be able to return to the museum.**
- **See if you are as clever as brainy Francis!**
- **Help Cleo keep an eye on Mr. Gluddery. He is not to be trusted.**
- **Help Clifford and Kevin, the twins, find each other.**
- **Help the party of ten solve Thoth's puzzles.**

IN THE TOWN

Our towns have wide streets for important processions and narrow alleys between the houses. The houses are several stories high with small openings to let in light and keep out heat. People sit on mats on the flat roofs to feel the breeze. They cook up there too.

Most Egyptians don't use money. They barter, or swap things, instead.

The lady holding a bowl of eggs came to the market with a fish to swap for eggs. The egg merchant didn't want the fish but the pot merchant did. Look at the stands and figure out what swaps she had to make to get the eggs.

IN THE DESERT

This is the desert beyond the fields. Ordinary Egyptians are afraid of the desert. They come only when they have to. The Pharaoh hunts lions here to show how strong he is.

Temples and tombs are cut into the rock here. Many Egyptians are buried in these tombs.

Four pieces of stone have fallen from the two statues being cut into the rock. Can you find them and figure out where they fell from?

AT THE TEMPLE FESTIVAL

Clifford! Where are you?

What's Mr. Gluddery doing behind there?

Temples are built as homes for the gods, and only priests and the Pharaoh may enter them. Once a year, statues of the gods are paraded around the countryside for all to see.

On these occasions there is a festival. Stands are set up to sell lucky charms and special food and drink. The drink has lumps in it, so people use straws.

There are two drink stands here, one selling drinks with green straws and one with red. Which stand has sold the most drinks?

AT THE PYRAMID

MAKING A MUMMY

AT THE PHARAOH'S PALACE

This is the Pharaoh's magnificent palace. We think of the Pharaoh as a god living on earth. Can you see him? He has a false beard and a gold crown. Pharaohs are usually men.

The Pharaoh has ordered these dishes for his birthday:

I'm going to try a little of everything.

You can't. The servants have forgotten to bring in one of the dishes.

Which dish is missing?

figs

bread

cucumbers

lettuce

grapes

roast chicken

cheese

honey cake